The JOURNEY BEGINS

Based on THE POLAR EXPRESS book and characters ™ & © 1985 by Chris Van Allsburg.
Used by permission. All rights reserved under International and Pan-American Copyright Conventions.
Published in the United States by Houghton Mifflin Company, Boston.
(s04)

www.polarexpress.com
www.polarexpressmovie.com

Library of Congress Cataloging-in-Publication Data

Richards, Kitty
The Journey Begins / adapted by Kitty Richards.
p. cm.
"The Polar Express."

"Based on the motion picture screenplay by Robert Zemeckis and William Broyles, Jr.;
based on the book The Polar Express written and illustrated by Chris Van Allsburg."

Summary: A boy who is eagerly awaiting a visit from Santa Claus accepts a ride
on a magical train headed for the North Pole.
ISBN 0-618-47795-0
[1. Christmas—Fiction. 2. Railroads—Trains—Fiction. 3. Santa Claus—Fiction.]
I. Zemeckis, Robert, 1952— II. Broyles, William. III. Van Allsburg, Chris. IV. Title.
PZ7.R387Jo 2004
[E]—dc22
2004005231

Manufactured in the United States of America
LBM 10 9 8 7 6 5 4 3 2 1

THE POLAR EXPRESS

The JOURNEY BEGINS

ADAPTED
BY
KITTY RICHARDS

BASED ON THE MOTION PICTURE SCREENPLAY
BY
ROBERT ZEMECKIS
AND WILLIAM BROYLES, JR.

BASED ON THE BOOK *THE POLAR EXPRESS*,
WRITTEN AND ILLUSTRATED
BY
CHRIS VAN ALLSBURG

DESIGN
BY
DOYLE PARTNERS

HOUGHTON MIFFLIN COMPANY, BOSTON 2004

Tick-tock, tick-tock. A boy lay in bed, listening to the clock. He was very quiet. He did not move.

He was also listening for Santa's sleigh
bells. He wanted to know if Santa was
really real.

Jingle, jingle! The boy sat up in bed. Could it be Santa? The boy got out of bed and tiptoed into the hall.

He looked downstairs. No Santa.
The jingle sound was just his dad's
Santa hat. The boy went back to bed.

The boy's parents looked into his room.
They thought he was asleep. His mom
gave him a kiss.

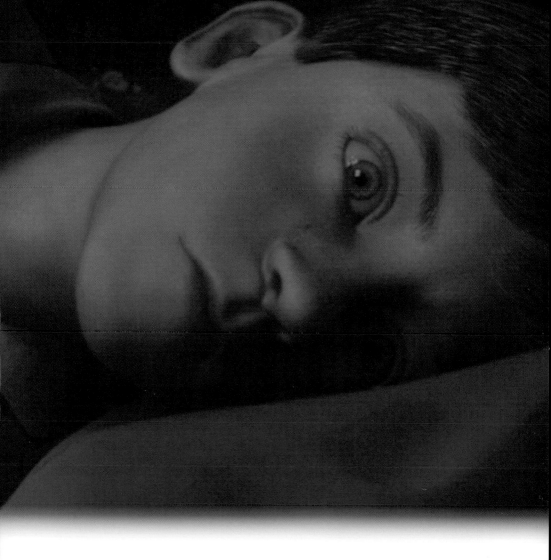

"He's out like a light," said his father.
"An express train could not wake him up."

The boy sat up
again. He looked out
his window. It was
snowing. *Tick-tock,
tick-tock*. He looked
at the clock. It was
10:20. Soon it would
be Christmas Day.
The boy yawned.
He was getting sleepy.

Jingle, jingle! The boy's eyes flew
open. It was 11:55. Five minutes
until midnight.

He stared at the clock. It wasn't ticking
anymore. It had stopped.

Just then the whole room began to
rumble. There was a loud roar and
bright lights.

The boy jumped out of bed and looked out the window.

He saw clouds of steam. He saw bright
yellow lights. He heard a long whistle.
What could it be?

The boy pulled on his slippers and his bathrobe. He ran down the stairs and threw open the front door.

The boy ran down the
snowy path and came to
a stop. The clouds of
steam disappeared. And
there stood a train.
A big train.

It was black and shiny. And it was as long as a football field.

The windows glowed yellow in the
cold, quiet night. The boy stared, his
mouth open.

The boy looked down his block. Just then a man in a uniform stepped off the train. He checked his pocket watch. "All aboard!" he shouted.

The boy looked up.

"All aboard!" the man called again.

He looked at the boy. "Well? Are you coming?" the man asked.

"Where?" the boy wanted to know.

The man looked closely at the boy.

"Why, to the North Pole, of course,"
he said. "This is the Polar Express."

"North Pole?" the boy said.

The man looked at his papers. The boy hadn't written Santa a letter. He hadn't put out milk and cookies. He needed to go to the North Pole! "If I were you," the man said, "I would think about getting on board." The boy didn't know what to do.

Should he get on the train, or go back
to bed? He stepped back. He'd go home.

But then he looked through the train's windows. He saw children laughing and singing. He climbed aboard.

The train moved faster and faster.
The boy was excited. Next stop, the North
Pole. And, the boy hoped, Santa Claus!